U0135960

———— ❧❧❧ ————

"It was the best of times, it was the worst of times, it was the age of wisdom, it was the age of foolishness, it was the epoch of belief, it was the epoch of incredulity, it was the season of Light, it was the season of Darkness, it was the spring of hope, it was the winter of despair, we had everything before us, we had nothing before us..."

Charles Dickens

———— ❧❧❧ ————

invisible (cities)

— ◆ —

waterfall #5
Invisible (Cities)

Publisher
Waterfall Publishing

Editor in Chief
Shauba Chang

Art Direction
Shauba Chang

Waterfall
10456 台北市中山區松江路84巷12號3樓
3F., No.12, Ln. 84, Songjiang Rd., Taipei City 10456, Taiwan
tel: 886 2 2381 0372
info@waterfallmagazine.com
www.hiwaterfall.com

ISBN 978-986-87162-1-6   680 NTD
Published in September 2012

index

我的人生就只是流水帳而已。在柏林房間裡面讀著精裝版的保羅奧斯特新作，日落公園。在出發前的早上收到Amazon的包裹，把書皮剝掉，裡面的硬殼是一片樸素的黑色布面，在書籍脊燙上SUNSET PARK PAUL AUSTER的times粗體。很厚一本，滔滔絮絮講述著看似零碎的小事，但卻又是這些瑣事構成了他們／我們的人生，這次的背景就是我們的時代，除了經濟不景氣之外還有關於歐巴馬與劉曉波等時事，雨從到柏林的第一個半夜開始下，依認真的那種，但即使在雨中，德國人依舊堅持不使用任何雨具，我無意間發現從住的地方走五分鐘就有間快照亭，老式連拍四格，閃光燈與沖洗劑，等了四分鐘之後吐出來的照片依舊沾附著藥水味，在飛機準備降落的十分鐘前，看見城市裡四處施放的小型煙火，從高空俯瞰也不過是一點一點的火花，在瞬眼間消散，倫敦有霧，從地鐵站走出來的時候，走進那些安靜巷道的時候，路燈在夜車裡的時候，就像是回家，永遠寫不完那些瑣碎的細節，像是地毯上永遠抖不乾淨的塵肩，日落公園剩下二十頁，結尾，讀完一本書，讀著好多個人生，作家的句子，有時候你想像，作家自己的人生，這個時候我在倫敦，那時候我在紐約第六大道與第十二街的交叉口，結果是在人行道上踩在童年，記于2010年生日五天後

booth by chance and it's just five minutes walk from where I live. Old style with four-frame photo paper, flash light and the developer, I waited for four minutes to get my photo while it's still a bit wet and had a chemical smell. Ten minutes before the plane landed, I watched the fireworks in the city from above, they're like tiny sparks everywhere, vanished in a blink. There's fog in London, it feels like coming home when I exited from the tube station, when I walked into lanes, when I saw the halation of the streetlights. You can't finish all those details, it's like the dust in the carpet that you never shake off all of it. Twenty pages left to the end of Sunset Park, the end. Reading a book and you're reading others lives at the same time. Sentences by the writer, sometimes makes you think he's talking about his own life. I'm now in London, by then I was standing at the intersection of 6th Ave. and 12th St. in New York, but after all I was in my childhood when I walked on the pavement. Written in five days after my birthday in 2010.

The Skin We Live in

Long Winters

Christian Göran

Taipei,
Silent Frame 9
Mao

Beijing Accomplice

ch. WeiWei
tr. Mavis Diamond

From noon, I rode the express for six hours to arrive at Beijing Southern Station just after dark. The platform was all fog. A few pairs of hands eagerly lit up. White smoke escaped between lips of various tongues, scattering over the train's headlights, turning into an orange dream that ate at travelers' heads. The air is thin and cold. I put on a purple wool cape, which is slightly torn in the inside. She had slept silently for 20 years in the closet at home, and I had brought it back to Time. By aging quickly, it has caught up to the present. I put her on to help her age a little easier. Train stations in China make me feel closer than possible to a migrant, like fish swimming against currents, eyes closed, blindly pushing forward. I put my luggage through the x-ray machine, it sucks it in and spits it out; just like that, I officially enter Beijing. Looking up from the crowd, I see a pair of Iceland blue eyes sweeping past the new subway signs and landing on me. I raise my hand.

Li Mo came from Moscow, but we met in London. Ouyang took me to a club where Li Mo was DJ-ing. That was pretty much the straightest club I have been to in the last few years: boys who were fresh college graduates with their Heinekens, trying to talk to girls wearing those little bare-back tuxedos. All the hormones on display made me smirk. None of them measured up to Ouyang though; she is both my woman and man, and my wish was to be broken by her. Ouyang introduced me to Li Mo when she was on her break, her huge headphones hanging around her neck . We awkwardly nodded at each other. I couldn't help but think of the story Ouyang told me the night before, she said they got shitfaced one night and a British girl took both of them home. She said she and Li Mo were like brothers so it wasn't really a big deal to them. It was the British girl, who got super excited, that made her nervous. "She was just too much." She wrinkled her nose.

"What do you think of Li Mo," Ouyang suddenly asked as we walked out of the club.
"Kind of cute," I said. The truth, too, I like people with curly hair and who are taller than me. Ouyang fell silent and suddenly and quickly and quietly said, "I'm afraid you'll sleep with her."

That's probably the most lover-like thing Ouyang has ever said to me. We entered the alcohol-soaked night, as usual Ouyang took off her jacket and put it over me. I used all kinds of tricks to try to get Ouyang to take me home, but she was afraid. She only kissed me, then pushed me in a depravity- and cheap perfume-filled night bus. At the end, neither of us surrendered to the other, and we just kept drifting in the ocean, on which floated pieces of our heartbreak.

Li Mo and I became close, after she came to China. She found me online, said she's shooting a film in Beijing, then 6 months later she decided to move there. I wanted to introduce her to people I know, but I don't know anyone as cool as she is. We occasionally exchanged emails, and we talked a couple times via skype when she had problems with some of her cross-cultural romance. I think my and her decision to live in Asia had something to do with wanting to escape. From a certain perspective, we are both living in each other's blind spots, where it's impossible for us to truly understand each other. And somehow that makes us both feel at ease. Li Mo is the Chinese name I gave her, actually she deserves a much wilder name, but I like the sound of the words Li Mo spoken aloud. It makes me think of the endless Trans-Siberian railway in the winter.

Beijing's subway isn't that much different from other metro systems in the world. Except there are even fewer people submit to looking at nothing, at gaining nothing. Outside, commercials rolled past us. The faster the train, the clearer they become. Li Mo leaned over and said she isn't a vegetarian anymore. Being a vegetarian in China is indeed difficult. "Even Blixa Bargeld, who was a vegetarian for 30 years, had to surrender to Beijing." She shrugged. We transferred twice and walked out of the station in the eastern part of the city. She walked me through a logjam created by two public buses blocking an intersection. None of the car would let the other one go. Honking everywhere. The driver got off the bus and cursed, and we snuck through the gaps between metal to the other side. Rumor has it that pollution combined with the changing season has covered the sky in an omnipresent haze, and through it, buildings after buildings look as if they were made out of paper. At the foot of these buildings, men women old young spit, sleep, play cards, cook, dry clothes, obliterating all boundaries between public and private. That is the time difference of Civilization, and because of that, the stubborn people of China seems especially avant garde.

"I love Beijing people. They are not afraid of anything." Li Mo opens the Chinese white wine in the room, pours me a glass, and downs hers. She knows better than I how to quickly make up for the trust and memory we'd never have. She mentions the film project she is working on, about three foreigners who dream of giving up their lives and start new ones in Beijing. She says Beijing is very fast, everyone is working on something new, which makes her excited. I told her I have been back in Taiwan for almost a year and had just finished a novel, but after it's done my insomnia started. It came from nowhere; it feels like everything of mine in the house was colluding to prevent me from going to sleep. When I think that all those things belong to me and no one else, I became breathless, my heart started to race, and I couldn't fall asleep no matter what. So all I could do was pack my bags and go to a foreign place to sleep.

"So you are in Beijing to sleep," she laughs.

I go to the balcony and don't answer, shutting the old, half-open wooden window. Winter is almost here, Li Mo says in about half a month, there would be heat.

"Ouyang told me about you before," Li Mo lightly sweeps her tongue along the rolling paper, closes one eye and lights up. "She said you sometimes gave her the impression that you were always going to disappear. It was a strong feeling, she didn't like it."

That's odd. I never thought Ouyang is capable of such fleeting, abstract words. I think of what Ouyang once told me about Li Mo.

"Li Mo is my accomplice."

We finish the Chinese white wine, and decide leave the old neighborhood to get beer at the little corner store downstairs. Almost dawn, the wide road feels barren, the air scratchy. I can't see very clearly, and almost fell a couple of times. Li Mo holds my hand. We are more tender than we imagine either to be, and that shocks me. Such an evolved type of love and tenderness; like what all cities in ruins are waiting to do, to give our deeply buried tenderness an opportunity. I wasn't genuinely moved, I only wish that everything in this moment looks beautiful. I know better than everyone else that our bodies don't belong to us, we have all been deceived by Enlightenment. Our bodies are nothing but carriers of love floating from this place to that, attracted to others, denied by others. Li Mo and Ouyang let me realize for the first time that bodies, being in the world, could sink, could perish, and as each others' accomplices, we have ties, and we have loyalty.

Soon, Li Mo is walking ahead of me. She stops, turns, and calls out my name, her right hand extended. I look at her, suddenly want to both live and die passionately. Then i pull her close, and deeply kiss her eyes.

北京同黨

威威

從正午乘快車六個小時到北京南站天黑沒下來已經一兩個小時，月台上全是霧，好幾雙手迫不及待點起了菸，相異語言的嘴吐出統一白色的烟、渙散在列車頭燈前成為橘色的夢吃掉旅人離去的頭。空氣薄且寒，我披上紫色內裡細細破開的褐羊毛斗篷，她無聲在老家衣櫥裡頭睡了二十年、被我帶回時間裡，現正趕上時代快速衰老，我想披著她使她老得輕鬆一些。中國的車站使人感覺自己無法更接近遷徙了，像季節潮流裡的魚，閉上眼無理推擠，我把行李抬上安檢輸送帶，任它吞進又吐出，然後正式進入了京城。穿過群魚仰頭看，李莫冰島藍的眼睛掃過簇新的地鐵燈誌轉向我，我舉起手。

李莫從莫斯科來，我們卻是在倫敦遇見的。歐陽帶我到一個舞會，李莫在裡頭當DJ。那大概是我近年到過最直的舞會，剛畢業的大學男孩拎著海尼根勾搭穿著露背小禮服的女孩搭訕，撲面而來的荷爾蒙使我發笑，他們哪裡比得上歐陽，她是我的女人與男人，被她捏碎是我的願望。歐陽介紹把大耳機掛在脖子上休息的李莫給我，我們糯糯地互相點了個頭。我沒法不想起前晚歐陽說給我聽的故事，說某天她們喝得很醉被一個英國女生帶回家睡，她說和李莫兄弟一場沒什麼大礙，但那英國女生反應熱烈讓她緊張，「她，太過頭了（She's just...too much.）。」她皺皺鼻子。

「妳覺得李莫怎麼樣？」走出舞會歐陽忽然問我。

「滿可愛的。」我說。這是實話，我喜歡卷髮而且比我高的人。

歐陽沈默了一段路忽然很快並且小聲地說：「我很怕妳會跟她睡。」

這大概是歐陽對我說過最接近情話的一句話。我們走進被酒精浸透的黑夜，照例歐陽把外套脫下來披在怕冷的我身上。我用盡各式拙劣的伎倆想讓歐陽帶我回家，但歐陽怕我。她只是吻了我，然後把我推上充滿腐敗與廉價香水氣味的夜間公車，最末我們誰也沒對誰臣服，各自離散在漂浮著心碎板塊的海洋上。

李莫和我接近起來，是她來到中國之後的事。她在網路上找回我，說她到北京拍片，半年後決定定居下來，我想過介紹朋友讓她認識，但我的口袋裡沒有和她一樣酷的朋友。我們偶爾通信，在她面臨異文化戀情困境時與她說過一兩次網路諮商電話，我想我與她的亞洲定居或多或少都埋有一點逃亡的意圖，並且某種程度說來各自身在真正認識對方的死角裡，這使我們對彼此感到安心。李莫是我給她取的中文名字，其實她本人值得更野的名字，但我喜歡李莫兩個字唸起來的聲音，那讓我看見冬天與漫長的西伯利亞鐵路。

北京的地鐵與世界各地沒有顯著的不同，只是人們少了更多望向虛空一無所獲的權力，窗外的廣告齊整流過眼睛，列車速度越快它們便越清晰。李莫挨著我說她不吃素了，在中國要吃素實在難。「連Blixa Bargeld吃了三十年的素也得向北京投降。」她聳聳肩膀。我們轉了兩次車之後走出東郊的地鐵站，她帶我鑽過被兩台公交車橫躺癱瘓的交通，所有汽車挺著胸膛不肯退讓，喇叭此起彼落，司機甩門下車撂下一串髒話，我們藉此從容自鐵皮縫隙之間游過。據說是空氣污染加上季節變換而生的漫天大霧讓大樓一棟一棟看起來全像紙紮的，男女老幼在大樓腳下馬路上吐痰、睡覺、打牌、煮食、晾衣服，沒有公私裡外的分別，那是文明的時差，任性的中國人因此顯得格外前衛。

「我愛北京人。他們什麼都不怕。」李莫打開房間裡的紹興花雕，給我倒了一小杯，自己也乾了一杯，她比我了解用什麼可以快速補足我們不曾擁有的信任感與回憶。她說起自己正在進行的拍攝計畫，是三個夢想放棄原本身分、到北京開始新生活的外國人，她說北京很快，每個人都在做一些新的事，那使她興奮；我跟她說我回台灣快要一年，剛寫完一本小說，但寫完之後開始沒有辦法好好睡覺。這障礙來得無聲無息，只覺得好像屋子裡所有屬於我的東西阻止我。想到它們不是別人的都只是我的，我就喘不過氣、心臟跳得胡亂飛快，怎麼也睡不著。所以我只好收了行李到陌生的地方睡覺。

「所以妳是來北京睡覺的？」她笑了。

我沒有回答她，起身走到陽台上，把半掩的老木窗整個闔上。冬天要到了，李莫說再過半個月就要開始供暖。

「其實歐陽跟我說過妳。」李莫伸出舌頭輕輕舔過紙捲好一根菸，瞇一隻眼點燃。「她說她有時候看見妳，覺得妳就是要消失的。那感覺很強烈，她不喜歡。」

真奇怪，我沒想過歐陽也會說出這麼飄忽的話。我想起歐陽有一次這樣跟我說過李莫：

「李莫是我的同黨。」

把花雕喝完之後我們決定下樓走出老社區，到轉角的小店買啤酒。接近清晨的大路沙沙的很荒涼，我的眼睛看不清楚、幾次差點跌倒，李莫牽住我的手。我們都比彼此想像當中更加溫柔，那使我驚愕，如此進化過的溫柔與進化過的愛，彷若所有毀壞中的城市等待著給我們深埋的溫柔一次機會，我沒有真正激動，我只希望一切在此刻顯得美好。我比誰都清楚人的身體不屬於自己，我們全都被啟蒙運動所欺瞞。身體不過是公共的載體借貸愛，此處流到彼處、被吸引被推拒。李莫與歐陽使我第一次意識行走江湖肉體會下沈會消亡，而我們同黨情存義長。

有一瞬間李莫走得快了，停下來回頭喊我的名字、伸出右手。我看著她，忽然想熱烈地活與死，就把她拉近，深深親吻了她的眼睛。

The Sun Also Rises

Jonny Cochrane

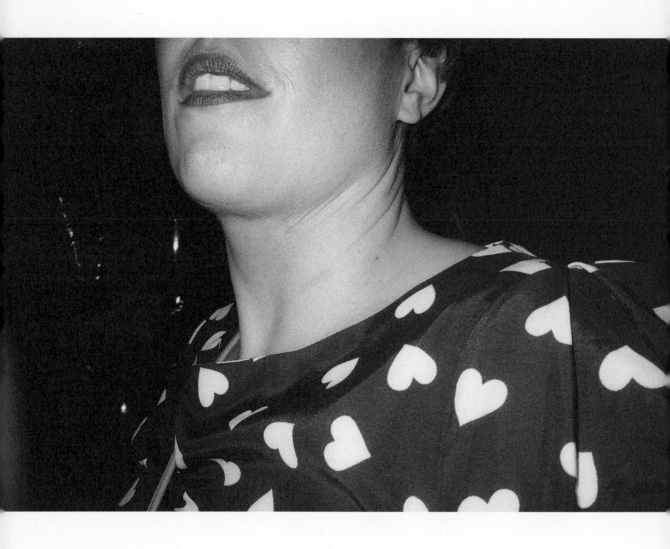

Property

———◆———

Backyard

Daisuke Yokota 横田大輔

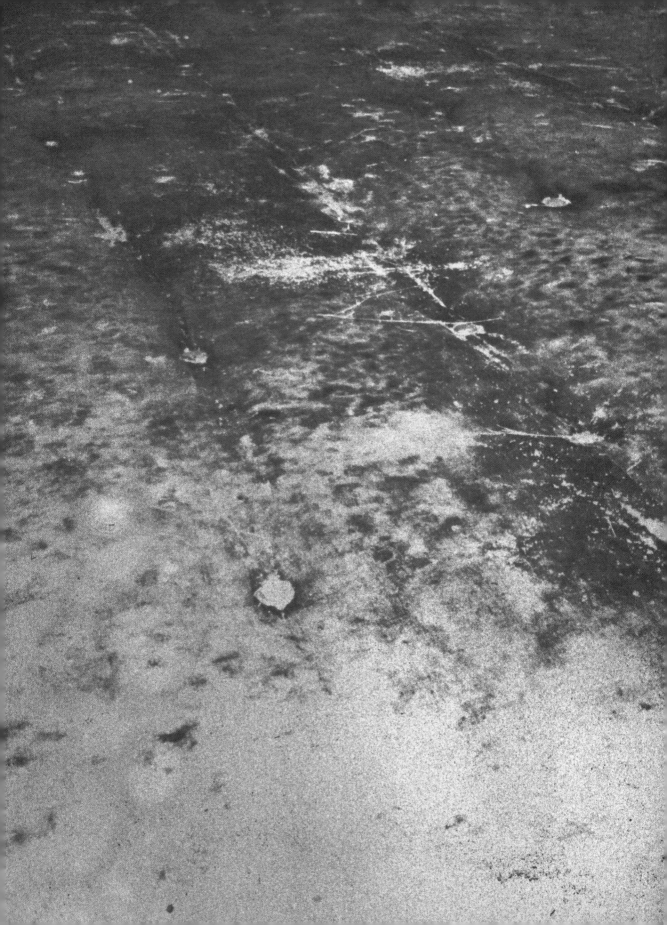

No. 5, Lane 14, Front Street

photography, footnotes *ETang Chen* 陳藝堂
text *YenWei Cheng* 鄭衍偉
tr. JiaRong Liao 廖家絨

Supporters guarding the Wang family stood arm in arm facing ample superior police forces.
守護在王家門前的人們以手肘互勾面對前方大量的優勢警力。

March 28, 2012

I went there at 5 am. I walked along the MRT tracks; shouts of demonstration in the cold, thin air sounded very distant. Demonstrators shouted with all their might, but yet so powerless. The police came in droves and set up iron gates, not letting people see what was going on inside. Later, the neighboring lanes were also blockaded by the police so that supporters of the Wang family could not get near. A few supporting college professors tried to get through layers of obstacles; the crowds responded with a thunderous round of applause.

7:50. Five households of the Wang family were banished by the Taiwanese government from their homes, where they have lived for more than a hundred years. The ancestral tablets they held in hand were as stiff as their facial expressions. More than three hundred supporting students were removed and lifted to the police vehicle like pieces of furniture or refrigerators. Not until the crowds were evacuated yearned the bulldozers for action, banging the walls as if to send threatening messages. The police jostled the crowd and asked for their IDs, not allowing people to take photographs. Vague shadows of people could be seen on top of surrounding tall buildings. They were the police, media and activists who got up there to witness the whole scene.

It was morning rush hours, streams of cars emerged. On the overpass nearby, drivers and bikers became lookers-on, blocking the traffic lanes. They then fueled up and drove away. Cameras were set high in order to get a better position, and then things happened.

In 2007, Le Young Construction Co. complied with the recent urban renewal policy launched by the Taiwanese government and expropriated lands for planning to build Wenlin Yuan. Because the two residences owned by the Wang family situated within the designated land, Le Young started to negotiate, hoping to obtain permission of the Wang family. There were, however, many disputes during the process. The Wang family put off their objections for more than two years, which is the legal time-limit for raising objections, and lost their case after entering legal procedures. The construction company sold all the pre-sale houses before they received the permission from all residents and posted advertisements accusing the Wang family as the "nail house" (people who refuse to sell their house and make room for development) that jeopardized the rights of other residents. Governmental regulations are not complete and lack flexibility; citizens do not even own the veto power, etc. In the end, the government actively assisted the construction company in demolishing private residences, of which the Wang family has full ownership, and strangely enough deployed over a thousand police officers to expel the supporting scholars and crowds.

In fact, even if the Wang family have not been completely honest during the negotiation and had negligence regarding legal procedures, Ministry of the Interior has expressed willingness to reconsider the decision; scholars and experts have also proposed a few other solutions. Nevertheless, the real reason why the incident drew so much attention from the Taiwanese society was because it pointed out significant problems in several different aspects. Major concerns of the general public were focused on whether private property rights were protected by the constitution. Some went further and stated that the government was "kidnapped" by construction companies and consequently deployed police forces to the scene. It neglected the vicious products with pre-sale problems and watched both parties of residents, who were all victims, attack each other. Fundamental problems in public welfare and legislation were yet rarely discussed.

The original idea of urban renewal was to improve the quality of living and safety in old street blocks concerning the whole city. However, the government only wanted to attract construction companies with high floor space ratio preference, which is to use increasing floor space ratio as an incentive for improving public welfare. The result of its passive attitudes led to the fact that landlords participating in urban renewal did not have to pay a penny to get a new house. According to the secretary director of The Organization of Urban Res, Peng Yang-Kai, it is a system that has never existed anywhere else. The cost of building houses is already high, and because of the high floor space ratio preference, construction companies tend to build more houses in popular areas and they even receive benefits from it. The old, deserted areas, which really needed renewal, are completely neglected. And due to difficulties of land consolidation, these urban renewal projects are often limited to small-area building renovation, not conforming to the original idea of large-area planning.

Recent news has stated that it is almost impossible for young people in Taipei to buy a house; disparity between rich and poor has repeatedly reached record high, and vacant rate in Taiwan is up to 19.3%. As far as national demand is concerned, basic living problems, which cannot be solved by simply building more houses and tearing down old ones in the name of urban renewal, are far more significant than real estate investments. Floor space ratio preference offered by the government should be public good and for the sake of improving living quality and safety in neighboring areas. It is absolutely illegitimate for construction companies to take all the benefits. Besides, current legal regulations concerning urban renewal are not transparent; local residents do not hold enough power to have a say during the developing process and can only allow consortiums and the government make the final decision. This way of dealing with public space is outdated. All of the problems listed above are the real hidden worries of public welfare.

Demonstrators in the Wang family incident may have been used; they may not have seen the whole picture, but they know that someone is using the greater power of exploit. They stood up because they did not want to remain silent when facing violence. They opened their eyes. The real principles are far beyond the law. The law is the bottom line, not the truth.

Former address of the Wang family after the forced demolishment. 王家被強拆後的俯瞰原址的地貌。

2012年3月28日

清晨5:00的時候我到了。順著捷運軌道走一小段路，抗爭呼喊的聲音在清冷蒼白的空氣中聽起來很遙遠。他們那麼用力，卻是那麼微弱。警察們陸陸續續就位，開始一層層包起鐵柵，不讓任何人觀看裡面發生什麼事情。接著，連周邊巷弄都被警力封鎖起來，不讓支持的人靠近。有幾名聲援的大學教授設法穿越重重障礙進去，獲得如雷的掌聲。

7:50，五個家庭被台灣政府從代代相傳居住一百多年的家裡驅趕出來。祖先牌位捧在手中，和表情一樣僵硬。三百多位聲援的學生像家具冰箱一樣被警察一一抬上車送走。人還沒走，怪手就蠢蠢欲動，恐嚇般搥打牆壁。而警方人員推擠，恫嚇要你出示身分證，不讓人拍照紀錄。四方高樓頂上可以看到人影在蠢動，是警察，是媒體，也有混上去觀望的運動人士。

上班的車潮湧現。一旁陸橋上，看熱鬧的駕駛和騎士堵塞車陣，又驅油門開走。攝影機高高搶位俯拍，一切就這樣發生了。

2007年，樂揚建設公司依循近年台灣政府推行的都市更新政策，徵收土地準備興建文林苑。由於王家五戶居民的兩棟自用住宅位於整個建設計畫範圍內，建商開始斡旋，企圖取得王家同意一起進行開發。然而在這段溝通過程當中出現許多爭議：王家拖延超過兩年法定期限才提出異議，進入法律程序之後敗訴；建商在取得產權同意之前就將預售屋全數售出，還刊登廣告汙衊王家危害多數人權益是釘子戶；政府法規本身不夠完備，缺乏協調彈性，民眾甚至沒有否決權力等等。事情演變到最後，政府不僅義務協助建設公司拆除民眾100%擁有所有權的私有住宅，還非比尋常出動1000餘名警力驅趕聲援的學者與民眾。

事實上，在這段斡旋過程中，即使王家表現不誠實，在法定程序上也有疏失，內政部還是曾經提出過重新審議的意見，學者專家也提出好幾個版本的解套方案。但是這整個事件真正引發台灣社會注意，是因為它凸顯出不同面向的重大問題。一般民眾多半關注的是私有財產基本人權是否受憲法保障。更進一步，會討論政府遭財團挾持出動警力協助建商，無視建商預售產權有問題的惡質產品，更放任兩

Neighbors across the street looked at the building site. The front door pathway has been blocked by the police.
王家對面鄰居向現場張望，他們門前那條通道已被警力封鎖。

造受害民眾相互攻擊。然而，更根本的公共利益與立法問題卻少有深入討論。

台灣政府推動都市更新，原始用意在於以整體市區大尺度面積為考量，改善老舊街區的居住品質和安全。然而政府態度消極，反而以高額的容積獎勵（一塊建地上面可容許興建的樓板面積）吸引建商投入，讓參與都更的地主一毛錢都不用出就可以換到新房子。根據專業者都市改革組織秘書長彭揚凱的說法，這是全世界前所未見的制度。建設房屋成本本來就高，這造成建商拼命建設原本就很熱門的地段還可以多拿獎勵，而真正需要更新的冷僻老舊地段完全無人問津。況且受限於土地整合不易，這些都更案往往侷限於小面積的建築整建，完全不符合大面積規劃的原始構想。

近年新聞報導常見台北年輕人完全不可能買房，貧富差距屢創歷史新高，全台空屋率高達19.3%等消息，就國家整體需求而言，基本居住問題遠高於置產投資，並不是齊頭式鼓勵都更多蓋房子就能解決。政府提供的獎勵容積原本應該是公共財，牽涉到街區的生活品質和安全，拿來送給建商獲利完全不合理。此外，現行相關法令制度不透明，原始居民在開發過程中缺乏參與決定權，只能受財團與政府擺佈，這種處理公共空間的思維也早已過時。以上種種才是公共利益層次的隱憂。

這次王家事件的抗爭者或許被利用，或許不一定看得見全貌，但是他們知道有人正在用更強大的力量進行剝奪。他們站出來，因為他們不想默認暴力，他們睜大眼睛。真正的原則遠遠超越法律，法律是底限，不是真理。

Streets behind the house of the Wangs. Police stationed at the base of Wenlin Yuan Construction Company, continued to remove supporters onto buses and "dumped" them to farther places.
王家後方馬路，警方駐守在文林苑建商的基地，持續將聲援者架上公車、準備丟到遠方。

After being expelled from the site, supporters could not leave freely. They were forced to get on the bus.
聲援者被驅離後無法選擇自行離開現場，被強制請上公車。

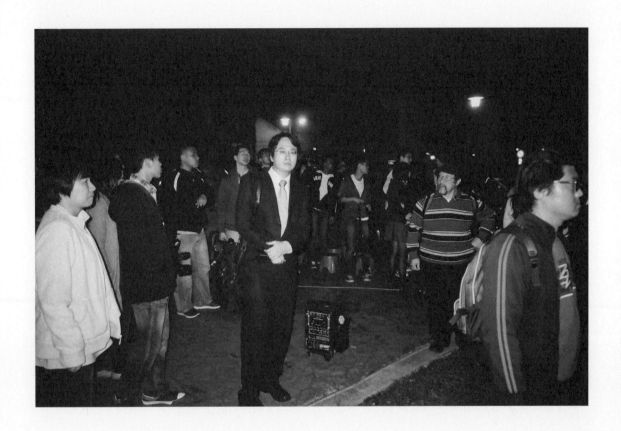

The night before the demolishment. People from all over the place gathered voluntarily on the plaza in front of the Wangs' houses.
被拆前夕，王家門前廣場上從各處自發性聚集來的人們。

One of the expelled supporters managed to escape the police's grasp and shouted: "Forced demolishment is against the law."
被驅離的聲援者中有人掙脫警方挾持，高聲疾呼「違法強拆」。

Chairman of Taiwan Association for Justice of Urban Renewal, Peng Lung-san, was a victim of urban renewal himself. He came to support the Wang family. While he was forced by the police to get on the bus, I tried to pull him away. The police then tried to drag me into the car as well. 都市更新受害者聯盟理事長彭龍三，他本身也是都更受害者，前來支持王家。正被警方強押送至巴士，我過去想把他拉走的同時警方也想把我抓上車。

A
Fleuneur
Who Collects:

Two Works
By

ChenHung Chiu 邱承宏

A carpenter and his Garden

installation
Taiwan cypress.soil.gold foil.Fossil building
dimension varies
2010

Note from the artist

From Buda and Pest, two old cities divided by the Danube, I looked for building fragments scattered around the churches in both cities. They were mostly left on the ground or in the gardens. Then I brought the fragments back to the museum in cart and washed them clean. After that, I placed the fragments in archival fashion on the self-made shelf with gold leaves and a wooden table. The source material for the oversized shelf and table came from the same material used for Taiwanese wooden architecture during colonial period. Through demolish and reproduction, it now takes on new function and meaning.

I decided to begin the journey from St. Stephen's Basilica.

以多瑙河貫穿的布達與佩斯兩座古都為中心，找尋散落在城中教堂周邊的建築碎片，祂們大都遺留在教堂地面上或花園裡，將這些碎片一車車搬運回美術館，並加以清洗乾淨，之後如同檔案一般陳列在貼有金箔的自製書櫃與木桌上。這些承載建築碎片的巨型桌子及書櫃木料來源，是台灣過去殖民時代木造建築的材料，經歷建築拆解再製而成，具備了新的功能與意義。

我決定從聖史帝芬教堂作為這趟旅行的出發點。

Confessional

installation
wood
1.4M(L)x1.2M(W)x2.1M(H)
2012

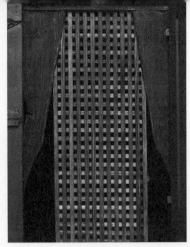

The 'Confessional' is a project ChenHung Chiu had been working during his artist residency in Paris. Everyday he promenaded on the streets to collect old furnitures abandoned by local residents. He tore them apart and cleaned them, according to different features and characteristic from these material, step by step, he built up a confessional-like installation. For him, the process of collecting not only connected him with the city and the citizens but also found him a way to create a theme: a closed form about monument. Which its source came from those forgotten objects around the city corner, and eventually got settled upon the the work as different file case and codes, trying to recall those memories and ghosts hiding behind the look of the city.

In the process, the artist used a found postcard which came with the furniture, he re-established a special relationship by using the sentences written on the postcard. He murmured the content towards all the objects he found on the streets, and install the sound within the confessional. He tried to connect all the individuals in this strange city with those words, from the family to the community, then all the figures gradually forgotten by the city would be summoned to where they should belong.
(tr. Shauba Chang)

《告解室》為邱承宏於巴黎駐村期間，每天從巴黎街頭蒐集居民丟棄在路邊的廢棄傢俱，再拆解洗滌之後，依據這些材料的特徵與屬性，逐步搭建出一間告解室造型的雕塑。對他而言，這種撿拾的過程除了連結城市與居民的關係之外，也試圖從中創造一個主題：一個關於紀念碑的封閉形式；它的來源是城市角落一些被遺忘的物件，最後如同各種檔案與符碼般建置在作品的表面，試圖喚回那些及隱藏在城市表面下的記憶與幽靈。

在這計畫進行的過程中，邱承宏透過一張伴隨廢棄傢俱拾獲而來的明信片，運用信中的文字與物件重新建立起一種特別的關係：邱承宏以悄悄話（murmur）的方式與這些拾獲物件敘述這則書信的內容，並將聲音安置在雕塑裡，從這字裡行間中，試圖連結陌生城市中的每個小個體、延伸至家、與社群，讓這些逐漸被遺忘的城市背影，重新喚回那原本屬於自己的地方。

Contents from the postcard:

Samedi 17 heures

Ma Chère petite Ninette,
Rien qu'un petit bonsoir en rentrant de
Miessier pour te dire que nous avons trouvé
grand mère Olympe très bien, aussi bien que
possible, elle était levée et l'appétit paraît
vouloir revenir.
Tu sais qu'un petit mot de toi lui fera
toujours plaisir, mais ne lui parle pas de
mon voyage à Nancy de jeudi, car je n'en
aie rien dit, à cause de ma petite tante qui
était à Jeuxey. Nous avons encore couru très
fort pour avoir notre train, il était en gare
et nous en bas d'un pont et canal, de l'autre
côté, en fin nous sommes arrivées, mais bien
essoufflées surtout cousine Jeanne.
Pour demain Dimanche un brin de mimosa
de Nancy avec en plus l'odeur de Liconille.

Mille bons baisers
Cousine Jeanne, tante Berthe, Fernande et ta
petite Denise.

星期六 17點

我親愛的小妮內特
只是想在從米耶席耶回程的路途上跟妳問候一
下，並且跟妳說我們覺得奶奶奧蘭普她已經好
多了，和以前能做的一樣，她已能夠起身並且
似乎也恢復食慾。
妳知道嗎，只消妳的隻字片語就能讓她常保開
心，但可別跟她提及我星期四去南錫度假，沒
跟她提這事是因為我那位曾在喬賽依的小姑姑
的緣故。我們拼了命的要趕上車，火車已經在
車站了，而我們卻還在運河與橋另一端的下
方，最終我們還是趕上了，不過大家都氣喘吁
吁，特別是你的表姊珍妮。
為明天的星期天，獻上一小段南錫的含羞草並
且還有琳可琳奈的味道。

獻上祝福的吻
表姐珍妮、姑姑貝特、費爾南德和妳的小丹斯

Affair

Gaze
into the Void

from the series work さすらい

Yuhki Touyama 頭山ゆう紀

24H (　　) People

ch. RenZhong Lin
tr. Zhang Sheng-chieh 張盛傑

Time's going on, (　)continue(s) his/her/their/its journey. Why can't (　)help entering department stores convenience stores supermarkets and fine art museums all the time? As feeling hungry, (　) must do so; once hiding in crowds of people, (　) would obtain a strong sense of security. Being fascinated with the intoxicating moment, just like the desire of stretching the index finger deep into the pharynx and meanwhile restraining vomiting. No watch, and the progress of time cannot be identified from the look of pedestrians as well. Why needn't (　) work? Or, why can't all (　) not here stop working? Almost needn't do so on Good Friday eventually. That vacant display window sees and is seen by thousands of eyes throughout the plaza. Nobody enters the church; postcards there are awkward and, after all, the church is not a masterpiece, even the souvenir store is hardly visited. On the day when shopping is impossible, (　) prefer(s) idling on the street or lakefront, or lying enjoying a sunbath, leading the lover by the hand and kissing him/her, letting dogs and kids poo and pee anywhere, eating sandwiches pickled cucumbers and drink beer, and listening to rock 'n' roll. This day, the business booms in the Chinese restaurant run by a Vietnamese in subway bazaar; observing humans of red color golden color deep brown color and white color use chopsticks with proficiency is much like appreciating Winnie the Pooh's donkey in the zoo. (　) would not love to meet the Asians that forget their own identities. Within one day only one thing can be done, so (　)forget(s) to buy the required items for Easter. To eat or not to eat the roasted chicken downstairs? This week (　)have/has already eaten four. Without eating roasted chicken (　) can't claim to be celebrating the Easter, and then finish(es) the remaining onions and mushrooms. A friend of (　)'s friend(s) brings a pot of soup, and smokes marijuana and does yoga at the kitchen corner. It is dawn.

Group travel results in waiting, not of the endless type. Some have a sense of time distinct from that of others, though; this is (　), and that is (　)that is (　)and (　), booting up and hibernating alternates from time to time. (　)finish(es) browsing through a book store in one minute while (　) study/studies merely one bookshelf for half an hour. (　) can see only one performance per day, (　) am/are/is still demanding more photography exhibitions. (　)never touch(es) spicy food yet (　) do(es) the opposite. Some (　) want to die but others don't. Oh, all drink coffee indeed, which can be bought on the street, from the subway stands café restaurant. All different. None of them remains sober when (　)are drinking the pink wine. The same for the call of nature; (　) pay(s) tips to go to the bathroom while (　)would endure for a whole day. Gradually (　) attempt(s) to walk his/her/their own way and gather at an appointed time, for example in a flea market. Nevertheless the experiment is a failure again: (　　)am/is/are still hesitating whether to buy a leather book bag, while others cannot stop eating dessert. Waiting, and waiting again. Here comes the luxurious supper in grand restaurants. Group travels invariably seem impressive; even a whole elephant can be swallowed, and eating others' left-over unnoticed becomes possible. Eating too much, some need exercise whereas others feel like going home to sleep. An odd number of travel groups have its pros and cons, but they are better than an even number of groups which are too jam-packed. Passing the time in waiting room, (　　)am/is/are constantly daydreaming. During the six-hour flight, all of (　　) sleep. In the raining airport are, luckily, free wireless Internet and free Starbucks due to the coupon provided by the airlines. With an inspiration, (　　) write(s) a passage in the diary: The visit to a prayer room and a fountain. The purchase of wine and perfume by credit card. The encounter with a female entertainer changing planes here, who (　　) can't even identify. The airplane takes off in the sunset, at last.

If lost, (　　) feel(s) relieved in particular. Leaping onto a train that gives announcements in an unknown language and setting out, (　　) do(es)n't get offended when getting on again, though having been ordered out the train halfway. Coming upon the Medieval Carnival taking place in the town beneath the Ferris Wheel, (　　) take(s) pictures with a witch and drink(s) bizarre wine plus a bunch of tulips. Running across the museum in maintenance; a worker, with a cigarette butt between his index and middle fingers, falls asleep on the scaffold, the billboard dropping in a flash. Encountering an old couple holding the hands of each other and jogging who run the red light encountering an artist peddling guitars who hangs himself/herself in front of a boutique encountering a kindhearted cherry tree that trips a cat encountering a deserted parking lot on fire. Bringing the great briskness from the loss of ability to read the loss of direction the loss of destination enables (　　)to walk much slower, all the way to a great glimmering snow-white lake and an alfresco bar. Leaning against the frozen wind, (　　) walk(s) on the lake surface feeling fatigued, enjoying the immense vacuum that is unheard of before. (　　)think(s) of having seen one movie, in which a frustrated middle-aged man goes to work the next day after karaoke. Stricken by sudden nostalgia (　　)continue(s) to walk, and from the unprepossessing boundary scurry out a great deal of wild dogs that attempt to attack (　　). Even if pretending not to be reckless (　　) still can't escape from this disaster. (　　) wring(s) (　　)'s neck(s), (　　) break(s) one of the arms, (　　)'s eyeballs are shattered and split, (　　) bleed(s) like a stuck pig. (　　) say(s) goodbye, grinning. (　　) jump(s) to the train with the wounds throughout the body, contented and leaving for another unaccountable destination. Receiving the jibes and points from people and pulled into the last one of the carriages by(　　), who determine(s) to fool with (　　). The clothes are torn, (　　)'s head(s) is/are pressed at the door to rub against the rail, but (　　) do(es)n't feel pain in the slightest. Not seen in the crowded after-working time, laughing, and brought away toward the endless night by the train.

二十四小時我們無時不在 _____

林人中

時間未滿，_____繼續上路。為什麼總是無法自拔走進百貨公司商店超市美術館，只要感到飢餓，就必須這麼做，一旦置身於人山人海，就會有無比的安全感。迷戀那接近昏厥的瞬間，就像把食指探進咽喉而同時抑止嘔吐的慾望。沒有手錶，行人的神情亦無法明確指認時間的進程，為什麼_____不用工作，或者，除了在這裡之外的所有_____為什麼都無法停止工作。終於在耶穌受難日那天，幾乎不用工作。那一間間空無一人的櫥窗，與遍佈廣場上數千隻眼目對望，沒有人進去教堂，教堂裡的明信片太醜了何況也不是大師蓋的房子連紀念品店都乏人問津。無法購物的日子寧可在街上在湖畔漫無目的的走，或是躺著晒太陽，與愛人牽手親嘴，讓狗與小孩隨地大小便，吃三明治醃黃瓜與啤酒，聽搖滾樂。這天，地鐵商場裡越南老闆的中國菜餐廳生意興隆，看著紅色金色深褐色白色的人嫻熟使用筷子好像在動物園欣賞小熊維尼的驢子。_____不喜歡遇到忘記自己是誰的亞洲人。一天，只能做一件事，於是忘了採買復活節所需用。要不要吃樓下的烤雞呢，這星期_____已經吃了四隻烤雞。如果不吃烤雞就無法說自己在過復活節吧，然後把剩下的洋蔥與蘑菇一併吃掉。_____朋友的朋友帶來了一鍋湯，坐在廚房的角落抽大麻做瑜伽。天亮了。

團體旅行的後果就是等待，不是永無止盡的那種。只是有的時間感總和有的不一樣，這個_____的，那個_____的那個_____的還有_____的，開機與休眠經常交錯。_____一分鐘就逛完書店_____半小時只瀏覽一排書櫃。_____一天只能只能看一場表演，_____還需要很多攝影展。_____不吃辣_____不吃不辣。有的_____想死有的不想。噢，全部都喝咖啡，路上的或是地鐵的攤販買的咖啡店買的餐廳買的都不一樣。_____喝粉紅酒的時候，全部都醉。上廁所也是，_____付小費_____願意忍耐一整天。漸漸便嘗試分開行動，約定一個時間會合，譬如說在跳蚤市場。實驗再度失敗，_____還在猶豫要不要買一個皮書包，有的不斷吃甜點。等待，又是等待。上館子豪華晚餐，團體旅行看起來總是好氣派，真的可以吃下一頭大象，也吃別桌客人的廚餘假裝神不知鬼不覺。吃太多有的需要運動，有的想回家睡覺。奇數的旅行團體總是有好有壞，但比偶數好偶數太擁擠。在候機室打發時間，_____都放空。六小時的航程，全部_____都睡覺。下雨的機場，幸好能免費無線上網，用航空公司提供的餐券喝星巴克。_____靈感來了寫一篇日記。參觀祈禱室與噴水池。刷卡買酒與香水。遇到女明星在這裡轉機，_____都認不出來是誰。飛機終於在夕陽裡起飛。

迷路的時候_____格外安心。跳上一輛聽不懂廣播的列車就出發，中途被趕下車再上車也不生氣。巧遇摩天輪底下的城鎮舉行中世紀狂歡節，_____與女巫合照並喝詭異的酒附贈一束鬱金香。巧遇維修中的博物館，有一名工人在鷹架上睡著，食指與中指夾著菸屁股，招牌瞬間掉落。巧遇牽著手慢跑的老夫婦闖過紅綠燈巧遇兜售吉他的藝術家在精品店前上吊巧遇友善的櫻花樹絆倒一只貓巧遇荒廢的停車場失火。帶著失去閱讀的能力失去方向失去目的地後一無所有的輕快，_____就能夠更緩慢，直到一大片閃著幽光的雪白色湖泊與露天酒吧。倚著冰凍的風，_____在湖面上行走，萬分疲憊。享受前所未有的巨大的真空。_____想起曾經看過一部電影，一名失意的中年男子唱完卡拉OK後明天繼續上班。忽然間十分想家。繼續走，就在無人在意的邊界竄出許多野狗，試圖攻擊_____。即便裝作毫不在意_____也無法避免這場災難。_____扭斷了_____頭、_____掉了一支手臂、_____眼球碎裂、_____血如噴泉。_____笑著說再見。_____帶著渾身傷口跳上列車，心滿意足前往下一個莫名其妙的地方。被人們指指點點，被_____拖進最後一節車廂，_____下定決心玩弄一番。衣服被撕裂，把頭顱放在車門外刷過軌道，一點也感受不到疼痛。擁擠的下班時間沒有人看見。笑著駛向無止盡的長夜。

Embody

ShihAn Chiang 蔣實安

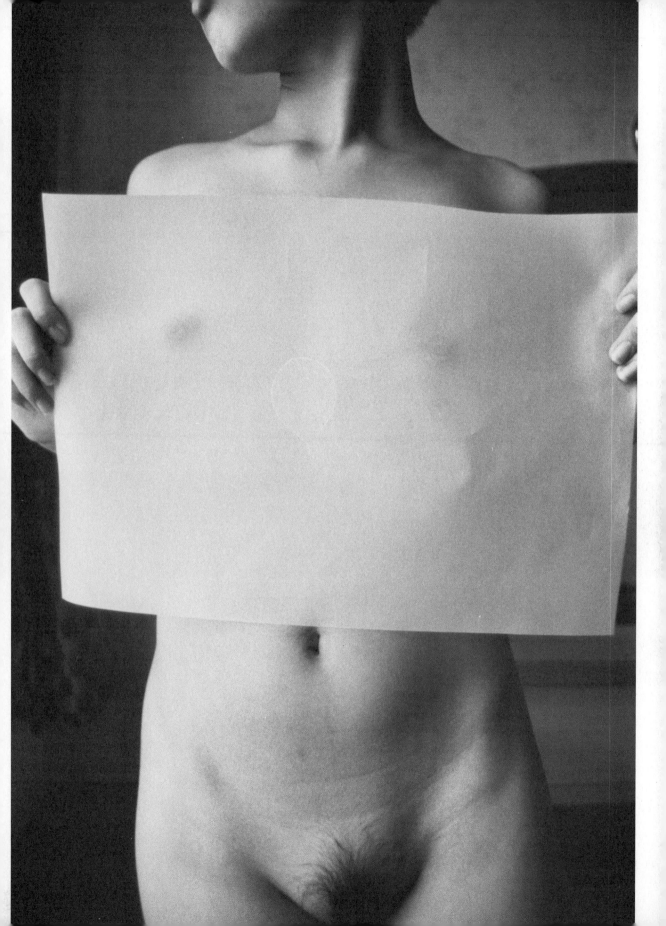

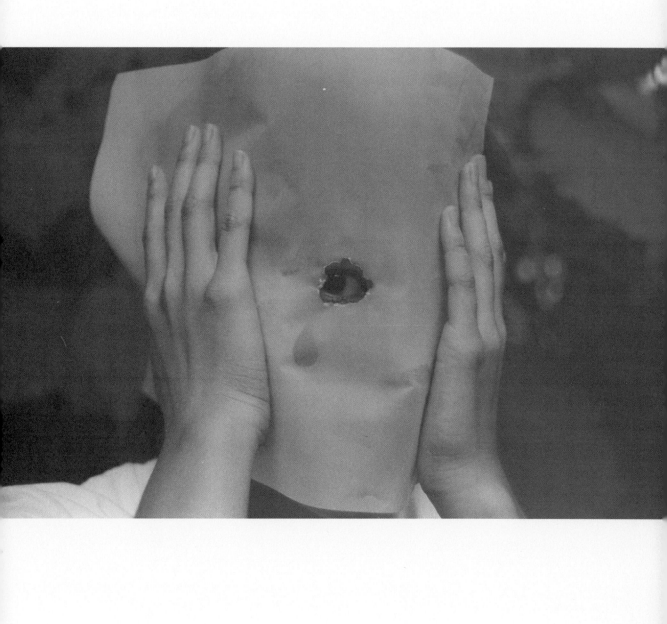

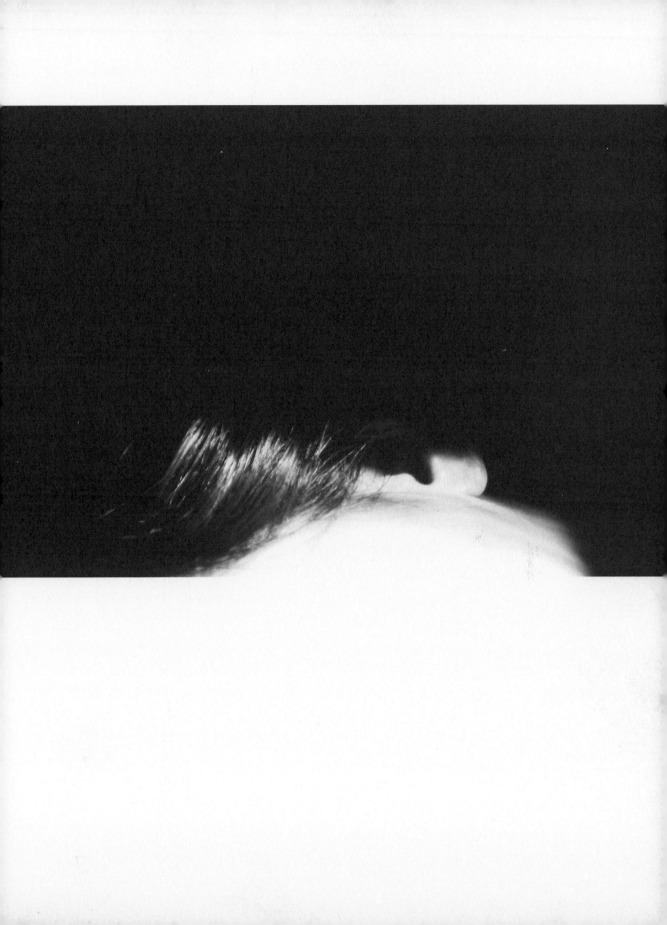

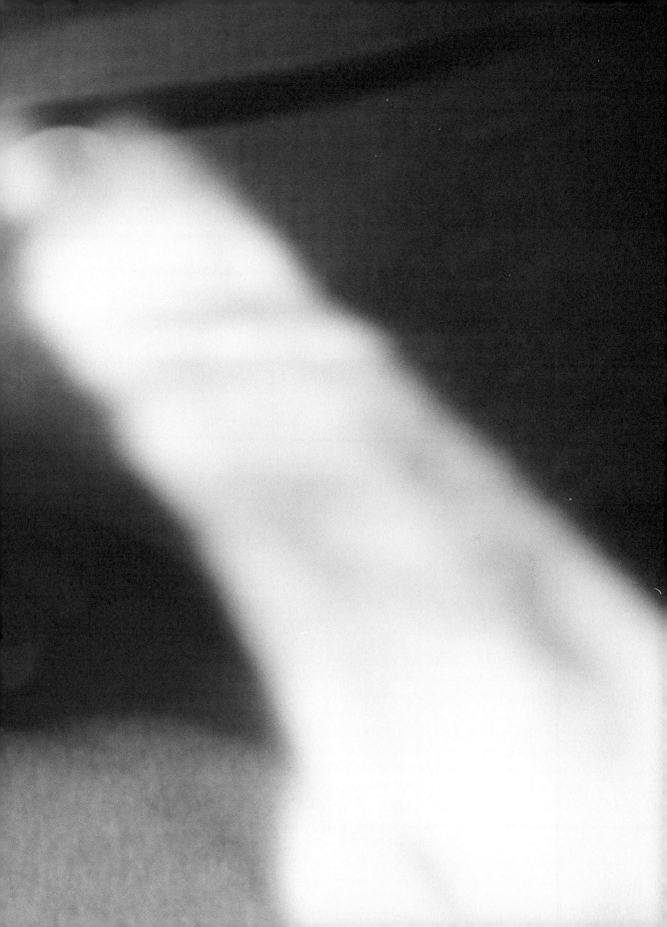

Fieldtrip

Berlin
Son Ni 兒子

BERLIN 2011/9

HOT DOG	HOT TEA	ICE CREAM	NATO WITH RICE	BITTER LEMON	TRADITIONAL BEEF MEAT	SPANISH COLD SOUP
ICE COFFEE	JAM FOR BEES	SOUSAGE	BREAD WITH HAM	PUDDING	BEER BEER	PLUM
BABOO TEA	KIMCHI HOT POT	SOY SAUCE MEATBALL	CAVIAR PINK + BLACK	KEBAB	INDIA FOOD	RICE PUDDING
THAI FOOD X3	SPICY WONTON	STEAM SPINACH	EGG + CREAM CHEESE + SMOKED SALMON	GERMAN FAST FOOD	PIZZA	? ? ? ?

Fieldtrip

Hong Kong

Chi Hoi 智海

Postscript:

Tristan Da Cunha

Lewis Chaplin
tr. YiChiu Chen

The Tristans is an ongoing, multi-faceted project involving direct discussion and collaboration with the people of Tristan Da Cunha - the most remote inhabited place in the world. Tristan Da Cunha is an active volcanic island no bigger than Manhattan, located in the middle of the Pacific ocean, a 14-day boat voyage away. The Tristans are British, using the pound sterling and the charming postcode of TDCU 1ZZ for the whole island - there are 250 of them, and seven surnames. Tristan Da Cunha now stands on the frontline in the battle against cultural hybridization and postmodernism, as they cling to the post-colonial remnant that is their island.

The project initially started from my involvement in both the fields of Anthropology and Photography, and the idea of attempting to bridge the gap between the two - most specifically the pursuits of representation and truth held within each. I am interested in how to represent and deal with notions of otherness and distance for a place I have never experienced, and how to handle a subject matter that is physically inaccessible. In my exploration and fascination with this place and its people, Tristan begins to feel more and more like a constructed fantasy, or an atemporal space rather than a physical entity of real people. I want to explore this abstract, dreamlike relationship with other worlds and other cultures, and the idealized visions held in faraway places.

The initial stage of this project evolved as a multimedia installation, utilising and playing with collage, found imagery and reference materials to evoke a sense of place and atmosphere, while abstractly revealing details of everyday life on the island. The second part is currently in progress and involves direct collaboration with the residents of the island. Included here is a selection of ephemera from the project, including original scans, collages and resources.

特里斯坦達庫尼亞群島

《特里斯坦人》是一個持續進行、帶有多重面向的計畫,與住在特里斯坦達庫尼亞群島上的人們親身進行的討論與合作。特里斯坦達庫尼亞是全世界最偏遠而仍然有人居住的島嶼,它是一座活火山島,面積不比曼哈頓大,位於太平洋的中央,需要一段十四天的船隻航行距離。特里斯坦人是英國人(British),他們使用英鎊,而迷人的郵遞區號「TDCU 1ZZ」則專屬於這座不過二百五十人、七個姓氏的島嶼。特里斯坦達庫尼亞目前正處在挺身反抗文化揉雜和後現代主義的前線,因他們墨守著後殖民的遺物-屬於他們的島。

這個計畫起初是與從我投身的人類學和攝影這兩個領域開始的,我抱著想法,想要嘗試將橫跨在二者之間的鴻溝給銜接起來 ——特別是對於再現的追求、各自存在於彼此其中的真實。針對一處從未經歷之地,我對於如何進行再現、論及該地的他性(otherness)和距離概念感到很有興趣,該如何處理這個事實際上難以到達的題材也是。經過探索,和對於這個地方、這裡的人們的著迷之中,特里斯坦開始逐漸變得越來越像一個建構出來的幻境,或者一個超越時序而存在的空間,而不真是一個有真人存在的實存物。我想要探究這份與其他世界或其他文化之間抽象、如夢一般的關係,以及探索這處被願景理想化的遙遠之地。

計劃起始於一件多媒體裝置,利用拼貼、拾獲的影像以及文獻材料來喚起一地的感知和氣氛樣貌,並同時透露這座島嶼上的每日生活細節。目前正在進行的第二個部分則牽涉了與當地居民的直接合作,在這裡所呈現的是這份計劃當中轉瞬即逝的一小部份選集,包括原始的掃描檔、拼貼物件、資料。

Mount Rowland

Oliver Dignal
tr. YiChiu Chen

Mount Rowland consists of photographic reproductions of black and white photographies. The pictures were specifically sampled from zoological photobooks and catalogues of natural history museums.

The question that evolves to the viewer, showing these pictures is, whether the photographed animals were alive or already taxidermied at the precise moment of photographic exposure. Some of the animals have become their protophotographic, skinned and remounted representation, shown in a museum, some were held in zoos. With this information the viewer starts doubting the tranquility of the image and imagines the object to be only frozen by its photographic documentation, but being alive, to be moving the next second. The mixture of photographies from museums and zoos creates this tension, that moves the viewer to visually wander between the motives, to compare and identify their original circumstances. No reflections in their eyes reveals their environment, a setting or cage, no scar or technical mistake defines their biological state. The partly low resolution, the structure of paper and theses photographie`s age seem to shrink the images even more down to their intense photographic quality.

Some say photography kills its motives, every moment dies within the second of its exposure. Here taxidermies are photographically resurrected in a believed vivid state, performing their last gesture of identity. Photography creates an equilibrium. All pictures are equally grey, equally still, equally frozen in time, the motives equally alive and dead, equally charged with a potential of movement, but substantially different.

羅蘭山

《羅蘭山》是一份黑白照片再製,這些照片取樣自動物學類的攝影書以及來自自然歷史博物館的目錄宣傳品。

透過展示這些照片、以向觀者進行提問,不管這些動物拍照時是否是活體、或者早已被製成標本好進行影像的曝製,這些動物已成為造相、被扒了一層皮、安置在屬於它們的再現體裡,出現在博物館中,有些則是在動物園裡。透過這些資訊,觀者開始質疑照片中所表露的凝止,並且想像被攝物只是被凍結在攝像記錄的當下,而實際上卻是活生生地、下一秒就會移動來去;這些混合了來自博物館、動物園的影像創造了一份強烈張力,讓觀者透過視覺揣想攝像的動機,並藉此比較、辨明它們原始的狀態。它們的眼睛當中看不見周遭環境的反射,是一個場景或是籠子,也沒有傷痕或是技術上的失誤來定義它們的生物狀態。某種程度的低畫素、紙張的質感以及照片顯露出的年份似乎都更讓這些影像皺縮至動物們充滿緊張意味的畫面質感上。

有些人說攝影殺死了它自身的動機,每個當下死於曝光時的那一秒鐘。在這裡,動物標本以影像之姿復活,栩栩如真,以它們最後的姿態進行身份演繹。攝影創造了平衡,每一張照片都擁有同樣的灰、同樣的靜滯、同樣的時光凍結,動機也同樣地既死又生,照片裡的動物同樣地保有著繼續動作的潛在可能。

但卻是根本上的大不同了。

Hundred Views
of
Fiction

HsinHui Kou 郭信輝

"Designed **( )** all brilliantly perfect, but they are dead. "

∗ **( )** : includes *A PIANO, GOOGLE TRANSLATE, AN ABANDONED AMUSEMENT PARK, LIGHTING OF A WELL-USE ROOM...*

I (mis-)use those existed thing in an unreasonable way, to create the multiple, compound aspect of them, like a conceptual reverse, to release common words into undefined.

Note from the artist

The name of this work starts from a personal experience in mis-using the new web tool : Google Translate. It has double meanings as "incorrect"and "in + correct", to criticize the implantation of mass media.

I tried to pick up many kinds of media messages,which including : news headlines , advertising slogans and the warning words on a cigarette box.... While import those messages into Google Translate, it remains only some fragmental details to recognize the original idea.

At the same time, artist also tried to invent a conceptual experiment, with the "Imitated Subtitle" as main character, I start to make sound, and try to find footages in cooperation .

In order to reverse a common cognition – that the visual image as main primary element, operating "music" or "dubbing" "subtitle".

background footages ⊠the work"Kindergarten Games"by Deng Nan-Guang , filmed in Taipei, during the Japanese Colonial Period, 1935.

作品來自於使用google translate這項新媒介的誤用經驗,英文名稱在字意上可視為 incorrect（不正確、錯誤），以及 in +correct（置入作為正確），表達對於媒體 操作行為的批判。

在這件作品中，我擷取了當下各式身邊媒體的訊息，包含：新聞標題、商業廣告 標語、和菸盒上的健康警語等等。並運用google translate翻譯這些訊息。呈現的 結果是片斷化的局部閱讀，原意只能經由想像推演，無法由字面企及。

同時，作者也企圖進行一場觀念實驗，以自行開發的「仿字幕」作為主角。開 始製造聲音，並進而尋找搭配的影像。試圖扭轉一般認定中影像作為主體，「配 樂」或「配音」、「字幕」作為輔佐的結構關係。

背景片段：1937年由鄧南光先生於日據時期拍攝的台北影像《台北幼稚園運動會》。

B-Side _____

PeiLing Tan
tr. Sauba Chang

The Listener Manual

What is any book on sound, both good and bad, but basically a visual representation of its purported object, where the only sound typically heard is the ghost-like voice in the reader's own head, silently intoning lines of text for an audience of one.'(Jim Drobnick, 2004)

I would like you to be aware that although you are looking at the text in this 'object-like' way, this conversation will only be meaningful unless you start to be attentive with the sound that you are hearing in your own head.

The Listener Manual is an instructional book that places the reader into various situations that they might encounter through listening. As hearing is not always conscious, instructions allow the body to be subjected to an intended listening experience, providing constant awareness to the environment one is placed in.

THE SILENT WITNESS

(1) Find a quiet location where almost no sound can distract you
(2) Hold a white bucket and slowly put it on your head.
 (Make sure the size is correct and you still have room space to breathe).
(3) Hold it for 30 seconds or more.
(4) Remove the bucket once you feel any discomforting sensation.

One of the only ways in which personnel based in Antarctica can train
newcomers to anticipate the sensation of visual and audio silence is
to put a white bucket over their heads in an attempt to simulate the
"nothingness" of a whiteout and the complete disorientation that occurs
as a result. (Barlow, 2010: 01 December)

Experiment on attentiveness to sound location, 1893

THE UNCONSCIOUS LISTENER

(1) Dig a small hole on the nearest ground that you can find.
(2) Insert a microphone into the hole, making sure that the switch is on.
(3) Amplify the sound in an empty room with loudspeakers.
(4) Stay in the space till you stop becoming attentive to what is being played.
(5) Leave.

Bruce Nauman has performed a similar instruction for a proposal-based exhibition, "Art in the mind", Allen Memorial Art Museum in 1969.
Bruce Nauman, Untitled, 1969

Drill a hole about a mile into the earth and drop a microphone to within a few feet of the bottom. Mount the amplifier and speaker in a very large room and adjust the volume to make audible any sounds that may come from the cavity.

GIUSEPPE CETRANGOLO

RICORDO

THE GHOST MACHINE

Hold it. Plug it. Pull it. Insert it. Push it. Turn it. Press it. Rewind it.
Play it. Pause it. Forward it. Stop it. Record it. Erase it. Unplug it.
Keep it.

Repeat.

This set of instruction is extracted from the instruction manual of 'How to
make the most out of your tape recorder'.

THE DOUBTFUL LISTENER

(1) Read this 30 Onomatopoeia.
(2) Imagine how they sound like in your head.

Bang
Bash
Beep
Burp
Boom
Buzz
Chirp
Click
Cuckoo
Hicc
Honk
Hiss
Hum
Knock
Murmur
Pop
Roar
Quack
Sizzle
Slap
Slash
Screech
Slurp
Snip
Splash
Squish
Whack
Whip
Whoosh
Zip
Zoom

Onomatopoeia is a word that imitates or suggests the source of the sound that it describes. Visual imageries is often conjured in one's head while trying to imagine the sound that these words suggests.

Nicholas Maes, The Listening Housewife (1656)

THE EAVESDROPPER

(1) Insert earpiece into both ears. Pretend you are listening to something.
(2) Appear to stay engrossed.
(3) Begin to listen to the conversation between the people around you.
(4) Do not make any eye contact with anyone.

"One can look at seeing, but one can't hear hearing." In the Green book, Duchamp question the role vision plays in the reception of his work. Sound is only made known to the person who listens, and in this case, the eavesdropper.

聆聽操作手冊

任何關於聲音的書，無論好壞，基本上都是它所指稱的對象體在視覺化後的代表。通常唯一被聽見的聲音只有在讀者腦中有如幽魂的話語，無聲地只為一名聽眾低詠那些文句。（Jim Drobnick, 2004）

我想提醒你的是，雖然你正看著這些物體化的文字模樣，但你必須開始專注於自己腦中聽見的聲音，之後的那些內容才能發揮作用。

聆聽操作手冊是一本導引書籍，分別將讀者置身於在聆聽上可能會遭遇的不同狀況。尤其「聽」這件事不總是有意識地進行，指令將使身體能進行有目的的聽覺體驗，並提供讀者對其所處環境的認知。

沈默的目擊者　　(1) 找一個幾乎沒有其他聲音可以讓你分心的安靜地點。
　　　　　　　　　　(2) 慢慢地把一個白色水桶套在你頭上。
　　　　　　　　　　　　（記得確認水桶尺寸可以讓你還有呼吸的空間）
　　　　　　　　　　(3) 持續三十秒或更久。
　　　　　　　　　　(4) 一有不舒服的感覺便將水桶拿開。

　　　　　　　　　　南極洲用來訓練新派駐人員去預知視聽死寂的方式之一，便是將白色水桶倒放在他們頭上，企圖模擬白茫世界的空無和完全失去方向感所產生的結果。（Barlow, 2010: 01 December）

無意識聆聽　　　(1) 在你所能找到最近的一塊地上挖一個小洞。
　　　　　　　　　　(2) 把麥克風放入洞裡，確定麥克風有開。
　　　　　　　　　　(3) 將收到的聲音在空房間裡用喇叭放出來。
　　　　　　　　　　(4) 待在那個空間直到你完全不會注意到究竟在放什麼。
　　　　　　　　　　(5) 接著離開。

　　　　　　　　　　1969年在AMAM，藝術家Bruce Nauman曾在提案形式的一個展覽《Art in the mind》上表演過類似的演練，作品名稱為〈無題〉。他在地上挖了一哩深的洞，將麥克風放入至離底部數呎。在一個偌大的房間安置擴大器與喇叭，並將音量調整至當下的任何聲響都聽起來像是從洞裡傳出來的。

鬼魂機器　　　　拿著。插電。拉。嵌入。推。轉開。按。倒轉。播放。暫停。快轉。停止。錄。消除。不插電。留下。

　　　　　　　　　　重複。

　　　　　　　　　　整套指示摘自於操作手冊《如何讓你的卡帶錄音機發揮最大效用》。

曖昧的聆聽　　(1) 讀完這三十個狀聲詞
　　　　　　　　　(2) 想像他們在你腦裡響起來會是怎樣

砰
叭
嗶
嗝
蹦
嗡嗡
喳
喀哩
咕咕
嘻
轟
嘶嘶
哼
叩
潺潺
啪
吼
呱
滋滋
拍
削
嘯
咕嚕嚕
喀嚓
潑
嘎吱
捶
咻
呼
滋
嘟嘟

狀聲詞是模仿或暗示它所形容的聲音來源的一種詞類。當我們試著想像那些詞表示
的聲響時，通常會伴隨著腦海中浮現的視覺意象。

───～～～───

竊聽　　(1) 把兩個耳塞都載上，假裝你正在聽別的東西。
　　　　　(2) 假裝很專心。
　　　　　(3) 開始去聽周遭人們的交談內容。
　　　　　(4) 不要與任何人四目交接。

「我們可以看到正在看的，卻不能聽見正在聽的。」 在綠皮書中，杜象質疑視覺
在接收他作品時所扮演的角色。而聲音只會被正在聽它的人接收，所謂竊聽，即是
如此這般。

It was no longer something that was waiting to leave. It had
become one of those things whose task is to remain,
to anchor the roots of some piece of the world. The
things that, when you wake up or come home, have
been watching you. It's strange. You go in search of
some amazing contraption to have yourself transported
far away, and then you cling to it with such love that *far,*
sooner or later, come to mean far from it.

Alessandro Baricco CITY . Translated by Ann Goldstein

拖車開始像其他東西一樣視停留為理所當然,而且要負責
把世界上某些片段的根留住。這些東西,在你甦醒或回家
的時候為你守夜。很奇怪,你去找一個很複雜的玩意兒
好帶你去「遠方」,你卻又愛憐地把它留在身邊以致於最
後,「遠方」也變得遙不可及。
亞歷山卓‧巴瑞科Alessandro Baricco《CITY》‧譯者倪安宇

———◆———